BLADES OF INDIGO - 1

Embers Before the Storm

YATHEESHA S PUJAR

Blades of Indigo-I

Embers Before the Storm

For information, contact :

yatheeshaspujar2810books@gmail.com

ISBN: 978-93-343-6017-2

First Edition : Septembre 2025

3 2

Why do you Love This?

Dear Readers, in the event that you take the poetic journey of "Blades of Indigo," I hope you find a well-forged story of sentiments and appreciation for the human experience.

It is the whispering of tales, nowhere more than by the tongues of silence: the cries that pained and angered the mind even when none heard them. So precious is this novel, my very first book, because it embodies exactly those things I feel about love: the strength it affords in connection with people and the resilience found even in the hardest downdrafts of life.

In getting acquainted with this story, I would love if people feel the healing waters of this story, inspire them on the journeys each character takes, and remind them that stories and experiences keep anyone from ever really being alone. A love story, a story of tremendous strength, an inspiring tale, and a tale where all my love for these was poured into every word. Thank you.

CONTENTS

ONE. THE PRICE OF PAPER AND MAPS 1

2. THE BLADE OF CERULEAN 9

3. WHEN EYES FIRST MET 17

4. BENEATH THE CRESCENT MOON 25

5. BLADES AND BOUNDRIES 33

6. A WAR OF WISPERS 39

7. TRAINING THE MIND, SHARPENING THE SWORD. 47

8. THE TIDES OF RESISTANCE 55

9. THE FLAMES OF THE AMPHITHEATER 63

X. THE PRICE OF DEFIANCE 73

PROLOGUE

The history of the twin kingdoms of Indigo and Cerulean was written in soot and scars long before the present era began. It was believed that even the stars turned away when the first blood was spilled at the Battle of Thorns in some distant year. One warlord seized the fertile land that would become Indigo, while another carved a kingdom into the icy mountains now called Cerulean-the first crime that would echo in the millennia to follow. No treaty lasted more than a generation. Love was impossible across the lines; trade was made under the watchful eye of both worlds, whilst peace was merely a delay between bouts of conflict. Cerulean rose to unmatched ranks of military prowess, its citizens having been hardened by the conviction that strength meant survival. Indigo, bruised but not broken, hence turned inward to ponder upon its philosophies, honing the art of diplomacy, espionage, and defense.

For centuries, the legacies of these conflicting movements crashed against each other like waves against a rocky shore. Entire villages have disappeared overnight; border towns have changed their flags with the seasons; and every person was raised with stories of fallen heroes and broken treaties. Among countless tales of war, however, came not a glimmer of hope- until the rise of a scholar-prince born beneath Indigo's moon and a warrior-princess trained in Cerulean flames.

Pangs of revolution mark the beginning of a new era. Indigo's court, though cultured, quaked under the burden of age-old wounds and a snoozing military. It's one heir, Prince Robin, who stood as the least likely in any naive mind to lead a rebellion or command an army- a boy more eloquent with scrolls than with swords. In the steel-blooded heart of Cerulean, Princess Rachel surged amidst statesmen and generals with an unmatched skill and loyalty unflinching.

Each knew nothing of the other, nor did each feel that fate, or love, would nay dare to crisscross the chasm their ancestors had dug. But upon such things history had little claim.

This is their tale-a tale of ashes and betrayal and a story of two hearts with an iron resolve that defied a millennium of hatred. This story unfolds in the last years of the ancient Yathee Era and thus seeks to usher in the present age.

This is the legacy that broke the curse.

This is how war gave way to peace.

And it began, not with swords, but with a meeting in a hall of marble and light...

Way before the 770s of the Yathee Era, the blood feud between Indigo and Cerulean had already solidified into blood and prophecy. Some say it began with a betrayal against a sacred relic; others place the blame upon ambition, pride, or even divine punishment. The truth is, perhaps, all of them-and none. Nevertheless, what mattered was that Prince Robin and Princess Rachel came of age in kingdoms that had known only war. Skirmishes were as common as snowfall. Hatred was inherited like titles.

And yet...

What neither kingdom could foresee was that love, unexpected and unrelenting, would become the fiercest weapon of all.

Thus, shall it be written- how the frost of war melted into the spring of unity. How two broken kingdoms healed not in conquest but in each other.

Integrate the love subplots into the entire series.

Key Characters

Prince Robin (of Indigo)

Description: Twenty-two years old, lean, long-limbed, pale as parchment. Has a mind suited for strategy and internal thought. His hands are often ink-stained, and his deep gray eyes reflect the maps he studies.

Aliases: The Paper Prince, Robin the Silent, Prince of Ink.
Skills: Highly intelligent strategist, adept at deciphering military journals, studying ancient treaties, and proposing theoretical conquests without bloodshed. Later trains in sword combat.

Family: Son of King Martin and Queen Maria.

Key Relationships: Elyan (steward and oldest companion).

Princess Rachel (of Cerulean)

Description: Twenty-one years old. Born during the Bloodlight Eclipse. Has frost-colored eyes. Often seen in silver-blue armor.

Aliases: The Blade Princess, The Undefeated, The Flame behind her father's throne.

Skills: Accomplished duelist, skilled in combat and devising flanking strategies. Known for precision and efficiency in movement.

Family: Second daughter of King Arthur and Queen Mary, younger sister to Princess Selene.

Key Relationships: Commander Draven (instructor), General Sorath, Minister Ilsera.

Elyan (of Indigo)

Description: Robin's steward and oldest companion, in his thirties, tall and gaunt with streaked gray hair. Has a long scar from the Battle of Lowfen Ridge.

Role: Advisor and confidante to Prince Robin.

Lord Varyn (of Cerulean)

Description: Cold-eyed and quiet Cerulean noble.

Role: Oversees secret gatherings and reports on Rachel's loyalty.

Sir Calder (of Indigo)

Description: Indigo's combat instructor, a man "carved from iron and raised in flame," with a milky left eye from an old battle wound.

Role: Trains Prince Robin in sword fighting.

World Overview

Kingdom of Indigo

Characteristics: Peaceful realm known for open fields, stone academies, and ancient observatories. Its strength lies in "scrolls" and "knowledge" rather than "swords" or "stone walls".

Capital: Castle Thalor - an elegant fortress with tall silver towers and jasmine-scented courtyards. Features a Library of Stone Echoes.

Monarchy: Ruled by King Martin and Queen Maria.

Emblem: Carved wolf figurine.

Kingdom of Cerulean

Characteristics: Militaristic eastern kingdom, known for conquest. Every child learns the Oath of Arms.

Seat of Power: Citadel Virelia - with jagged skyline, high towers, and blackstone barracks.

Monarchy: Ruled by King Arthur and Queen Mary.

Sigil: A lion beneath a crescent moon.

World Summit of Yathee Era 7730

Purpose: A peace gathering involving various nations.

Attending Nations: Cerulean, Elarien, Thornevale, Indigo (Host), Taria, Velstorm, D'Yorr (Observers).

Key Events and Plot Points

Prince Robin's Studies: Robin spends his days studying maps, military journals, and ancient treaties, earning him monikers like "Paper Prince".

Princess Rachel's Reputation: Rachel is a celebrated warrior, having outdueled lieutenants and devised successful military strategies.

The World Summit: Robin and Rachel are designated representatives for their respective kingdoms at a crucial peace summit.

Internal Pressures: Both Robin and Rachel face scrutiny and pressure from their royal families and advisors regarding their interactions, with fears of compromised loyalties.

Converging Interests: Despite their kingdoms' animosity, Robin and Rachel find common ground in their desire for genuine peace and understanding, transcending political rivalry.

Training and Trials: Robin begins sword training with Sir Calder to prepare for unforeseen challenges. Rachel faces a public duel against Commander Veylen to prove her loyalty to Cerulean.

Unveiling Deception: Robin and Rachel independently discover that information is being manipulated and forged to provoke conflict between Indigo and Cerulean.

Shared Hope: They recognize that their shared goal is to prevent betrayal and bloodshed, opting instead for "hope" and unity.

BLADES OF INDIGO - I

Embers Before the Storm

ONE

THE PRINCE OF PAPER AND MAPS

Wing I: The Kingdom of Scrolls

In the far reaches of the western realm, where indigo hills curved like sleeping giants and ancient rivers flowed with the hush of memory, stood the quiet kingdom of **Indigo**. Unlike the war-born empires to the east, Indigo wore no scars of battle. Its strength lay not in swords, but in scrolls — not in walls of stone, but in walls of knowledge.

The kingdom was a patchwork of open fields, stone academies, and ancient observatories, where monks studied stars and scribes copied the treatises of dead philosophers. There were no war drums in Indigo, only the steady rhythm of turning pages.

At the heart of this realm sat **Castle Thalor**, a fortress more elegant than defensive, with tall silver towers and courtyards scented with jasmine. It was within these walls, atop a marble staircase and beneath a domed ceiling painted with constellations, that **Prince Robin**, only son of **King Martin** and **Queen Maria**, spent his days — and nights — surrounded not by knights, but by maps.

Wing II: The Paper Prince

Robin was twenty-two, and the court had stopped expecting him to grow broader shoulders or take up a sword years ago. He had the body of a scribe — lean, long-limbed, pale as parchment — and the soul of a strategist. His hands were always ink-stained. His eyes, a deep gray that seemed to reflect the maps he so often stared at, rarely met another's directly unless he was making a point.

He wasn't a coward — just... internal.

Quiet, careful.

Where others in the court sparred or hunted, Robin deciphered military journals or studied ancient treaties. He had read the entirety of the **War Scrolls of Ilaron**, memorized the flawed invasion paths of the Elarien Empire, and once proposed a theoretical conquest of the southern isles without shedding a drop of blood. That last one had earned him laughter in the war room.

Still, the Queen often said Robin had *"a mind that could undo empires if he ever learned to shout."*

But he didn't shout.

He reasoned.

He stood now at the center of his chamber, which resembled more a war library than a royal bedroom. Stacks of open scrolls leaned precariously on desks. Miniature carved soldiers, painted in shades of red and blue, were positioned across three different map tables. The air smelled of wax, parchment, and dried lavender — the scent Queen Maria insisted all her son's rooms be filled with, in hopes it might "*soothe the mind.*"

Robin wasn't soothed. Not today.

Wing III: The Name on the List

His eyes scanned the list on the desk before him.

World Summit of Yathee Era 7730: Attending Nations

Cerulean (Confirmed)

Elarien

Thornevale

Indigo (Host Nation)

Taria, Velstorm, D'Yorr (Observers)

And under Cerulean's entry, scrawled in the neat, clipped handwriting of the royal courier:

Representative: Princess Rachel, second daughter of King Arthur.

Robin stared at that line for a long time.

Rachel.

The name struck like a whispered secret he wasn't supposed to know.

He had read her name before — dozens of times, in reports and diplomatic exchanges, in military records and intercepted rumors. She was a living legend. At sixteen, she had outdueled three Cerulean lieutenants in ceremonial combat. At seventeen, she helped break the Siege of Belcrest by devising a flanking strategy that scholars still debated. And now, at twenty-one, she was representing her kingdom at the world's most delicate peace gathering.

Robin had never seen her.

Not in person.

He'd seen a painted likeness once — all cold eyes and silver-blue armor, standing atop the walls of Cerulean's capital like a war goddess. But paintings were never real. They couldn't show laughter, or doubt, or softness.

He wondered what she looked like when she wasn't carrying the pride of an empire on her shoulders.

He also wondered if she had ever heard of him.

Probably not. He wasn't famous. Not beyond the intellectual circles of the Western academies and the dusty halls of political theory.

He was the **Paper Prince**. That was what the Cerulean dignitaries called him. He knew — he'd seen the intercepted letters.

"*Robin the Silent,*" one had called him.

"*Prince of Ink,*" said another.

"*Better suited to libraries than to thrones*."

He should have been angry.

Sometimes he was.

But more often, he was just... tired.

He didn't want to be anyone else. But sometimes he wished they could see the value in the boy who stayed up until dawn drawing theoretical escape routes for cities he'd never visit. Who could tell you how to dismantle an invading army without ever lifting a blade?

Wing IV: Conversation with Elyan

A knock at the door pulled him from his thoughts.

"*Enter*," he said.

The door creaked open and in walked **Elyan**, his steward and oldest companion. Elyan was in his thirties, tall and gaunt, with hair that had once been black but was now streaked with gray. A long scar ran down the side of his neck — a gift from the Battle of Lowfen Ridge. He leaned heavily on a darkwood cane, though he rarely complained about it.

"*You've read the list twenty-seven times,*" Elyan said dryly. "*Care to make it an even thirty?*"

Robin gave him a look. "*It's important.*"

"*She's just a girl.*"

"*She's a symbol,*" Robin corrected. "*And not just any. Rachel of Cerulean. The Blade Princess. The undefeated. The flame behind her father's throne. If she's attending, it means Cerulean isn't just interested in diplomacy — they want to test us.*"

"*You mean test you.*"

Robin didn't reply.

Elyan walked over, picked up a carved wolf figurine — Indigo's emblem — and turned it over in his hand. "*You think she'll try to provoke you? Outwit you?*"

"*I think,*" Robin said carefully, "*that she's been taught all her life that weakness must be eradicated. And Cerulean sees Indigo as weak.*"

Elyan grunted. "*We are weak. Militarily.*"

"*Which is why I need to be ready.*"

Elyan smirked. "*You're planning a war with a woman you've never met.*"

Robin finally smiled. "*Isn't that what love is?*"

Elyan nearly dropped the figurine.

Robin's grin faded. He looked down at the map before him. "*I don't know her. But I've read her. Her movements. Her decisions. Her mind. I... I respect her. And I'm afraid of what she might think of me.*"

"*You're not a soldier,*" Elyan said, more gently. "*But you're more dangerous than most of them.*"

"*That doesn't matter to people who only count swords.*"

"*Then make them count something else.*"

Robin looked up sharply.

Elyan nodded toward the blank corner of the map. "*You've got nine days. Use your mind. Build something unexpected. Be the prince they never saw coming.*"

Wing V: The Star-Stained Balcony

That night, Robin couldn't sleep.

He stood alone on the high northern balcony, the stars spread wide above him.

Below, the kingdom rested, peaceful and oblivious.

From here, he could see the distant hills that marked the border. And farther still, in his imagination, the mountain-flanked realm of Cerulean — where Rachel might be training beneath a moonlit courtyard.

He didn't know her voice.

He didn't know if she was cruel, or kind, or curious.

But something told him — whatever happened at the summit — he would never be the same.

And maybe, just maybe, neither would she.

2

THE BLADE OF CERULEAN

I: Kingdom of Iron and Fire

The sun rose blood-orange over the jagged skyline of **Cerulean**, casting long shadows between the high towers and blackstone barracks of **Citadel Virelia** — the seat of power in the eastern kingdom. The morning air crackled with the clang of steel and the bark of orders, echoing off the stone like thunder in a canyon.

This was no kingdom of peace.

Where others sang lullabies, Cerulean sang of conquest.

Where others, every child here knew the **Oath of Arms** before they learned to read.

And even in such a nation, one name stood tallest among giants.

Princess Rachel. Born in the winter during the Bloodlight Eclipse — her first cries swallowed by the howling of wolves — her arrival was marked with prophecy and contradiction. Some priests called her the blade that would carve Cerulean's next empire. Others feared she would be the fire that burned it all.

Even Rachel wasn't sure which one she'd become.

Wing II: Trail by Blade

"*Anyone else?*"

A wooden crack rang out on the training grounds.

Rachel drove her practice sword straight into the chest plate of a knight nearly twice her size. He stumbled back, grunting, armor dented.

"*You dropped your guard,*" she said coolly.

"*Yes, Your Highness,*" the man gasped.

The training circle fell quiet.

Not in fear.

In reverence.

At twenty-one, Rachel had never lost a match.

She stood in armor crafted to fit her precisely — lightweight Cerulean steel engraved with moon sigils. Her braid was tight, her stance poised, her frost-colored eyes sharp enough to slice pride.

Every movement she made was precise. Efficient. Beautiful.

Her instructor, **Commander Draven**, stepped forward.

"*You're ready,*" he said.

"*I was ready last month,*" Rachel replied flatly.

"*The summit will test more than your sword.*"

"*I know.*"

"*Do you?*"

Draven's gaze was steady. "*You've never needed politics. On the field, your blade speaks. In a court, silence and glances can betray kingdoms.*"

Rachel turned, walking away across the stone.

"*Then I'll learn another kind of warfare.*"

Wing III: The Crescent Throne

The **Hall of the Crescent Throne** glimmered with steel and silver banners. Cerulean's sigil — a lion beneath a crescent moon — rippled in the morning light.

King **Arthur** sat atop his throne like a mountain of stone, silent and solid. At his side stood Queen **Mary**, sharp as ice beneath velvet. And beside her — perfect in posture — was Rachel's older sister, **Princess Selene**, the firstborn and political heir.

Rachel entered without flinching.

"*You sent for me,*" she said with a respectful bow.

"*We did,*" Queen Mary answered. "*You will represent Cerulean at the World Summit.*"

Rachel raised an eyebrow. "*Why not Selene?*"

Selene replied, voice crisp: "*I've been tasked with securing the eastern front. You're the presence we need in the west.*"

"In other words," Rachel murmured, *"I'm the threat Indigo needs reminding of."*

King Arthur's voice rumbled. *"You are not there to fight. You are there to remind the world of Cerulean's strength — through poise. Through presence."*

Selene added, *"Through silence. Let them underestimate you. Let them squirm in your shadow."*

Rachel's mind swirled. She had led armies. She had fought monsters. She had survived trials that killed others.

But this — a summit of words, masks, strategy — this was new.

And **Indigo** waited at its center.

Wing IV: The Paper Prince

"He was not the prince Cerulean mocked."

That night, Rachel sat alone in her study, moonlight painting her desk with silver.

Scrolls littered the surface — maps, tactical reports, wax seals. But one parchment lay apart.

A **classified file** from Cerulean's espionage division.

Subject: Prince Robin of Indigo

She read it carefully.

No confirmed combat experience

Noted strategist with a high academic reputation

Referred to as "Paper Prince"

Last seen at the Grand Library of Indigo

No romantic affiliations
Studied Cerulean military doctrine

One entry caught her off guard

Authored an anonymous paper in a neutral journal proposing an alliance based on shared failures, not shared enemies.

She had read that essay.
Twice.
She hadn't known it was his.
Robin wasn't the silken puppet Cerulean painted him as.
He was something else.
Something… unexpected.
Something **dangerous** is in his way.

Wing V: The High Tower and the Question

"What if victory didn't come from breaking him?"

Later that night, Rachel stood on her high tower balcony, wrapped in a plain robe. Her sword rested at her side, untouched.

Below, the palace simmered with quiet tension. Troops changed shifts. Forgeries crackled. Wind sang between battlements.

Above — stars, sharp and cold.

They looked different than those in the West. Closer. Wilder.

She looked at the moon and whispered silently into the night:

What does Indigo see when they look at me?
A threat?

A monster?

A war machine?

And what would ***Robin*** *see?*

A rival?

A storm?

Or... something else?

Would he cower? Would he mock?

Or would he surprise her?

Cerulean had taught her to conquer.

To dominate.

To win.

But here, in the stillness of starlight, a whisper bloomed in her mind:

What if winning didn't mean breaking him?

What if it meant... understanding him?

She turned back inside.

Her reflection caught briefly in the glass — moonlight on steel, the second daughter of Cerulean.

In nine days, she would step into enemy land.

Not with an army.

Not with fire.

But with her **name**.

And face the only prince who had ever made her question who she truly was.

3

WHEN EYES FIRST MET

Wing I: Banners and Tension

"For the first time in three decades, Indigo's capital was alive with voices from every corner of the world."

The city of **Indigo** bloomed with silk and sound. Flags of ten nations fluttered above rooftops like a festival of color. Dignitaries poured into the streets, market stalls shouted in every language, and musicians played lutes under bright summer skies.

Inside **Castle Thalor**, all shimmered with ceremonial elegance. Polished marble reflected golden sunlight. Crystals dangled from chandeliers like captured starlight. Indigo-colored silks draped the ceilings, and servants moved like clockwork spirits.

Prince Robin stood near an ivory pillar in the grand hall, watching. He stayed half in shadow — not hiding, but observing. The delegations entered, each a world unto itself:

- **Tarians**, cloaked in feathered elegance.
- **Velstorm**, stern and gilded.
- **Elarien**, walking like the wind given human shape.

And then — the air shifted.

Cerulean.

Silence followed their arrival.

At the front, radiant in blue and steel, came **Princess Rachel**. Her armor shimmered like flame-kissed ice. Her expression was unreadable — a storm held in place by sheer discipline.

Robin's heart stopped.

This was her.

Not a painting. Not a report. Not a rumor.

Their eyes met.

And in that instant — for one breathless flicker — the summit became irrelevant.

Wing II: Impressions and Intrigue

"But instead of feeling superior, she felt something else — curiosity."

Rachel had faced beasts, warlords, and traitors. She had stood on the front lines and watched grown men quiver.

But the boy by the pillar was unexpected.

He was... understated. Formal robes, disheveled hair, eyes too heavy with thought. He did not look like a prince of the empire.

But he looked.

And she saw something in him — not fear. Not ambition. But storms.

Robin looked away first.

She noticed.

And instead of judgment, a strange **curiosity** unfurled in her chest.

Her feet moved, but her mind lingered behind.

Wing III: A Voice That Carved Silence

"May our swords rest. May our minds speak."

The opening ceremony unfolded, layer upon layer of pageantry and pleasantries.

King Martin spoke kindly, his voice like gentle rainfall — polite but without thunder.

When **Prince Robin** was called to speak, Rachel leaned in.

No scrolls. No guards. Just him and his voice.

"We meet here not as allies, nor as enemies, but as the inheritors of a world cracked by the ambitions of our forebears..."

He did not shout. He did not declare.

He **invited**.

His speech resonated not through force — but **restraint**. Through clarity. Through calm conviction.

Rachel's lips curved, just slightly.

For the first time since entering Indigo, she smiled.

Wing IV: Words in the Garden

"A silence of weight, like two stars drifting closer in orbit."

The summit's first evening brought warmth and gentler airs. Beneath silver lanterns and flowering vines, dignitaries mingled in practiced civility.

Robin stood beneath a pergola of starfruit vines, a glass of spiced water in hand. He watched the sunset, nerves thin but contained.

Then—

"Impressive speech."

He turned.

Rachel.

Their first real moment — unarmored by duty, untouched by protocol.

Their conversation unfolded like a duel in slow motion:

"*You speak like a poet.*"

"You move like a storm."

"Is that flattery?"

"Just observation."

Barbs softened into insight. Jabs turned into revelations.

He asked her why Cerulean sent *her*.

"Because I can end a war with a single glance. Or start one."

He asked what she wanted here.

She hesitated.

"I don't know yet. But... I want to understand what makes you so dangerous without lifting a sword."

This time, he held her gaze.

"Maybe we're both more dangerous than we appear."

Wing V: The Moment That Changed Everything

"Not love. Not yet. But the beginning."

The night buzzed with diplomacy.

But beneath that buzz, something ancient stirred between the warrior and the thinker.

Two minds shaped by different worlds.

Two souls weighed down by expectation.

Two hearts that had never truly been seen — until now.

Rachel smiled.

And for one suspended breath, the world stood still — not because of threat, or ceremony, or alliance.

But because two people, trained never to yield, saw something in each other worth softening for.

It was not love. Not yet.

But it was the beginning.

4

BENEATH THE CRESCENT MOON

Wing I: The Choreographed Storm

"Every word a blade hidden in silk."

The summit continued like a play rehearsed a hundred times.

Morning meetings.

Midday debates.

Evening feasts.

Every hour, every conversation, cloaked in calculated gestures and polished phrases. But beneath the gilded diplomacy, tension simmered — not yet boiling, but close.

At the eye of this quiet storm, Robin and Rachel lingered in orbit.

They hadn't spoken since that garden night.

No letters. No words.

Only glances.

And each time their paths crossed, their eyes found one another — brief, subtle, electric.

It wasn't courtship.

Not yet.

It was something quieter. Something *aware.*

Wing II: Dreams and Moons

"He dreamed of her in ink. She searched for him in moonlight."

Robin began dreaming.

Not in romance, but in metaphor — war tables made of parchment, battlefields drawn in charcoal, and always across from him: Rachel, waiting, unreadable, just beyond reach. She was becoming part of his thoughts. His doubts. His equations. Rachel, too, was changed. She found herself drawn to balconies at night, staring westward beneath Indigo's twin moons. Watching. Waiting.

For what?

She didn't know. A message? A figure? An answer?

She had survived beasts, blades, and betrayals.

But nothing had prepared her for this new enemy: hope.

Wing III: The Moonlight Garden

"The garden was shaped like a crescent — a sanctuary for those who didn't belong."

On the fifth night, Robin couldn't sleep.

His thoughts swirled — summit proceedings, ancient treaties, and fragments of her voice. He read and reread reports, but nothing stilled his mind.

So, he wandered.

Barefoot. Silent.

Through the ancient halls of Castle Thalor, until he found himself before the Moonlight Garden — a secluded crescent of marble and nightbloom, veiled in hedge and memory.

He entered.

And found her.

Rachel. Standing alone beside the fountain.

No armor. No throne. Just her — wrapped in soft blue, braid falling over her shoulder, dagger at her hip.

She turned, unsurprised.

"*And you often wander restricted gardens at night?*"

"*Only when sleep refuses me,*" he replied. "*This place helps me... untangle things.*"

"*Then perhaps,*" she said, stepping aside, "*it's a place for two thinkers.*"

Wing IV: A Place for Two

"Do you believe peace is possible?"

They stood in silence, moonlight painting silver trails across the water.

Rachel's voice broke the stillness.

"*Do you believe peace is possible?*"

Robin hesitated. Then nodded.

"*But not easy. Not quick. There's too much blood between us. Peace requires trust, and trust takes time.*"

Rachel looked down.

"*Time is a luxury Cerulean doesn't offer easily.*"

"*You were sent here to intimidate,*" he said.

"*And yet here you are, asking about peace.*"

She studied him.

"*Maybe I'm just trying to understand the enemy.*"

"*Do I seem like an enemy?*"

"*You don't fit into any box I was trained to expect.*"

Robin smiled softly.

"*Neither do you.*"

Their masks had cracks now. And the people beneath them began to speak.

"*So, what are we then?*" she asked.

"*Exceptions,*" he answered. "*Ghosts of a better world that hasn't happened yet.*"

Wing V: The Space Between

"The silence wasn't awkward. It was sacred."

They sat side by side on the marble bench.

Close.

Not touching — but **close enough to feel**.

Rachel's voice was a whisper.

"*I used to think love was weakness. That made you hesitate. Lose focus.*"

"*And now?*" Robin asked.

She looked at the moon.

"*Now I wonder if love is the only reason we survive the wars we start.*"

Robin was silent.

Then:

"*I believed logic could fix everything. That if I just mapped it right, I could prevent the pain.*"

"*And could you?*"

"*No. But maybe... with the right person, I could try again.*"

They turned toward one another.

And in that moment — in the soft dark beneath ancient stars — something changed.

Not a kiss.

Not a vow.

But a promise.

A quiet recognition.

Two pieces that were never meant to fit.

And yet — somehow — did.

Wing VI: The Whispered Name

"When they parted, it was not with touch, but with memory."

Rachel rose first.

No parting words.

Just a final glance, slow and lingering — like the closing of a door that might one day open again.

Robin remained.

Alone beneath the crescent moon.

He traced his hand along the bench where she had sat.

And then, finally, whispered what he had held in his chest since the first moment she looked at him:

"*Rachel.*"

5

BLADES AND BOUNDARIES

Wing I: The Rhythm Beneath the War

"War. Peace. War again."

The world had a rhythm — one that pulsed beneath the treaties, beneath the diplomacy, beneath the masks. Kingdoms danced to it sometimes hand in hand, more often with blades concealed behind silks.

But in the shadow of the **Yathee Era 7730 Summit**, something strange was beginning.

For the first time in centuries, the rhythm skipped. Faltered. Hesitated. Something was forming — fragile, cautious — between Rachel of Cerulean and Robin of Indigo.

And just as it began to take shape…

The rhythm snapped back.

Wing II: The Council of Sharp Words

"Diplomacy is war with open hands."

Day Five of the summit. The Council of Defence Allocation convened. In the Crescent Chamber, beneath arched windows and watchful eyes, every attending nation gathered for what was — in form — a dialogue about defence.

In truth, it was a proxy battle between Cerulean and Indigo.

Rachel sat cloaked in royal elegance, the warrior hidden beneath embroidered robes. Robin sat opposite, still haunted by the previous night's memory — her voice in the garden, her honesty like a blade that cut through doubt.

But now, their battlefield was words.

"*We propose Cerulean command structure oversee the Vale of Serith,*" said **Lord Vallon**, his voice laced with polished threat.

Gasps. Murmurs.

Indigo's sovereignty — insulted.

Robin stood, calm and steady.

"*Silence often signals assent,*" he said, turning Cerulean's inaction into their undoing.

Then — boldness.

He stepped to the map. Placed a token.

"*Neutral ground patrol. Overseen by both Cerulean and Indigo. Equal voice.*"

A third path.

Rachel's expression barely shifted — but inside, her thoughts stormed.

He wasn't just resisting. He was leading.

The meeting adjourned, unsettled but not broken.

Robin had shifted the board again.

And this time, the world noticed.

Wing III: Moonfang and Midnight Voices

"Your stance weakens after the third spin."

The courtyard behind the north tower was silent, save for the singing blade in Rachel's hand.

Moonfang danced in practiced arcs.

Strike. Twist. Cut.

Again. Again.

Until—

"*Your stance weakens after the third spin.*"

She froze.

Robin stood in the shadows. No guard. No armor.

Just him.

Rachel's pulse quickened. Sheathed her blade.

"*And your arrival is poorly timed.*"

"*I couldn't sleep,*" he said. "*Neither could you.*"

They spoke as blades do — indirectly. Precisely.

"*You didn't stop Vallon,*" he said.

"*I represent Cerulean,*" she replied. "*To oppose him publicly would be weakness.*"

"*You're not weak.*"

Their eyes met.

Not as prince and princess. Not as a strategist and soldier.

But as two people caught in a quiet storm.

"*What are we doing?*" she asked.

"*I don't know,*" Robin whispered. "*But when you speak, I want to listen. And when I speak... I hope you hear me.*"

Wing IV: Philosophy and Fire

"Let's build a place where wanting is allowed."

They circled each other — not in combat, but in confession.

Rachel moved, blade still in hand.

"*You believe peace is a theory.*"

"*And you believe it's conquest,*" Robin replied.

"*It's how I was raised.*"

"*So was I — to trust paper over people.*"

They were two teachings, two wounds, standing face to face.

And for once, not trying to win — just trying to understand.

"*What if our people find out?*" she whispered.

"*Our families?*"

"*They'll try to end it,*" Robin said.

"*Then why are you still here?*"

"Because you're the first person who makes me want to fight for something more than survival."

Silence again.

But it was full, not empty.

Rachel's voice dropped into something almost reverent.

"You're dangerous, Prince Robin of Indigo."

He stepped closer.

"So are you, Princess Rachel of Cerulean."

Wing V: The Line They Did Not Cross

"Something passed between them stronger than touch."

They didn't kiss.

There was no hand taken. No promise whispered.

But in that moment — lit by torchlight and bound by everything unsaid — something ancient and powerful took root.

Not lust. Not diplomacy.

Recognition.

That night, Rachel sat alone with her blade across her knees.

She looked down, but saw his eyes.

Not fearful. Not soft.

But strong in a way that shook her.

And for the first time in her life…

She wished for a world that could hold them both, not as weapons, but as something more.

6

A WAR OF WHISPERS

Wing I: The Cerulean Conspiracy

The mask of peace, peace no longer wore a crown.

It wore a mask.

And behind that mask, war sharpened its claws.

The grand corridors of Castle Thalor, once filled with open debate and laughter, had grown quieter, colder. The shadows between the marble pillars seemed to stretch longer. Servants moved more carefully. Courtiers whispered with downcast eyes.

Because while the meetings still carried the banner of diplomacy, every delegate could feel it: Something was changing.

Wing II: The Cerulean Conspiracy

In Cerulean's private quarters, a gathering was held in secret.

Lord Varyn, cold-eyed and quiet, stood at the head of a narrow table flanked by several Cerulean nobles, including **General Sorath** of the eastern front and **Minister Ilsera**, a sharp-tongued woman known for her ruthless interpretations of the Cerulean code.

"*Rachel is wavering,*" Varyn said, voice low and clipped. "*Her loyalty is compromised.*"

"*She still argues for Cerulean,*" Ilsera replied. "*Even in today's session, she corrected Indigo's interpretation of the Serith Accord.*"

"*She corrected it,*" Sorath interjected, "*but not with conviction. She hesitated. The fire in her tone is gone.*"

"*She trains late into the night,*" Varyn said. "*And Prince Robin trains now too — with guards, with weapons. Why?*"

The silence answered the question.

"*He's preparing for something,*" Varyn said. "*And he's pulling her with him.*"

Ilsera narrowed her eyes. "*If they unify…*"

"*They won't,*" Varyn interrupted. "*We'll stop it before it becomes more than a whisper.*"

Wing III: The Watchers of Indigo

In Indigo's war chamber, Queen **Maria** paced beside a wall of battle charts and sealed missives. Beside her stood **Commander Elyan** and King **Martin**, whose expression remained unreadable.

"*I've allowed this—this curiosity—with the Cerulean girl,*" Maria said. "*But it must end.*"

Martin spoke slowly, deliberately. "*It is no crime to speak with a guest.*"

Maria turned. "*It is no crime. But it may be a fatal mistake. Cerulean has never sent a daughter to a summit without reason.*"

"*She is reason enough,*" Elyan said cautiously, "*for war or peace.*"

Maria stared at Robin's name etched on the court scrolls.

"*If he is falling for her,*" she whispered, "*we are already losing.*"

Wing IV: Quiet Surveillance

Robin wasn't blind to the tension.

He saw the way his mother's eyes lingered longer than usual. How the guards near his chambers shifted in number. How the reports arriving on his desk now came half-redacted. His training sessions were interrupted. His scrolls began vanishing.

It was quiet surveillance.

The kind of pressure that didn't bruise the body — only the spirit.

That afternoon, he cornered Elyan in the old scriptorium.

"*Are they watching me?*"

Elyan didn't answer directly. He only said, "*Your strength has always been your mind, Robin. But now, minds alone won't win this.*"

Robin sighed. "*What are they afraid of?*"

"*Losing you,*" Elyan said. "*To her. Or worse — through her.*"

Robin was silent for a long time.

Then he said softly, "*I would never betray Indigo.*"

Elyan placed a firm hand on his shoulder.

"*I know. But they fear what you might give up for peace. Even love can look like surrender to those who know only war.*"

Wing V: A Letter from Home

Rachel, too, was beginning to feel the pull of a thousand unseen hands.

In her chambers, she received a sealed letter from her sister Selene.

Rachel,

Father has not spoken openly, but Varyn's reports reach him nightly. I urge you: remember who you are. Your heart is your own, but your crown belongs to Cerulean. Be careful.

—Selene.

Rachel folded the letter without a word.

Then burned it in the candle flame.

Wing VI: The Library of Stone Echoes

That evening, Rachel walked the halls of Castle Thalor cloaked in silence, slipping past guards, past courtiers, down toward the

Library of Stone Echoes — an ancient part of the palace rarely visited, its vaulted rooms filled with echo chambers and forgotten tomes.

She wasn't surprised when she found him there.

Robin sat at a long stone table, surrounded by scrolls and old ink jars, the weight of strategy thick in the air. He didn't look up when she entered.

"*Your guards let me pass,*" she said.

He finally looked up. "*I told them to.*"

She approached, setting her gloves on the table beside a partially unrolled map of the Northern Ridges.

"*They're watching us,*" she said.

"*I know,*" Robin replied. "*Yours too?*"

Rachel nodded. "*More now than ever.*"

Robin leaned back, eyes tired. "*They think we're plotting.*"

Rachel folded her arms. "*Aren't we?*"

He smiled faintly. "*Not against them. But maybe for something bigger.*"

She sat across from him, hands resting on the cool stone. "*Tell me, then. If you could change everything — Cerulean, Indigo, all of it — what would you do?*"

Robin looked at her, not as a princess, not as a political opponent, but as **Rachel** — the girl who stared at moons and danced with blades.

"*I'd start with us,*" he said softly. "*One truth between two liars.*"

Rachel looked down.

Then up again.

"*I want to trust you,*" she whispered.

"*Then do,*" he said.

"*But I don't know if I can trust myself.*"

Silence.

Then Robin leaned forward, voice low.

"Let's give them something to truly fear, then. Not betrayal. Not bloodshed. But hope."

Wing VII: Dangerous Laughter

Later that night, a servant witnessed something they would never forget.

A prince and a princess — rivals by birth, by crown, by oath, sitting side by side, heads bowed over a single scroll, fingers nearly touching.

And when the servant turned away, they heard laughter.

Soft.

Warm.

Dangerous.

In the shadows outside, **Varyn** watched from a high balcony. And smiled grimly.

7

TRAINING THE MIND, SHARPENING THE SWORD

Wing I: The Breaking Sun

The morning sun did not rise kindly over Castle Thalor.

It broke the horizon like a blade, fierce and glaring, casting long shadows across the courtyard stones. A new day had dawned—one that would not be softened by diplomacy, nor comforted by the illusions of control.

For **Robin**, it was the day his world would begin to shift.

Not by words.

Not by maps.

But by the slow, painful discipline of the sword.

Wing II: The First Lesson

The training yard of Indigo's eastern barracks had been silent for years. Used only by retired guards, it had fallen into a kind of ceremonial emptiness—a place meant more for visiting nobles to watch than for real war-hardened bodies to sweat in.

But not anymore.

Robin stood at its center now, stripped of his courtly robes. He wore a plain tunic, soaked already in sweat, his hands trembling lightly from the weight of the wooden training blade in his palms.

Across from him stood **Sir Calder**, Indigo's bluntest—and most feared—combat instructor.

Calder was a man carved from iron and raised in flame. His left eye was milky from an old battle wound, and his voice had the rasp of someone who had never once uttered anything frivolous.

"*Again,*" Calder said.

Robin lifted his blade.

Swing. Parry. Step back Lunge.

Too slow.

A blow cracked across his forearm.

Robin grunted, dropping to one knee, the sword falling from his hands.

Calder didn't move.

"*Again,*" he repeated.

Robin picked it up.

Not because he had to.

But because he **chose to**.

Wing III: Rachel on Trial

Elsewhere in the castle, Princess **Rachel** knelt inside the stone meditation chamber reserved for Cerulean's royal emissaries. The walls were carved with runes of balance and clarity. It was meant to be a sanctuary.

Today, it felt like a cage.

Standing before her were General Sorath and Minister Ilsera. Their expressions were as sharp as the cold ceremonial daggers they wore at their sides.

"*You're being watched,*" Ilsera said without pretense. "*Your behavior has raised questions.*"

"*I haven't broken protocol,*" Rachel replied.

"*No,*" Sorath agreed. "*But you've bent it. In subtle ways. Unspoken ones.*"

Rachel rose to her feet. "*Am I to be condemned for speaking with another delegate?*"

Ilsera narrowed her eyes. "*You're not being condemned, Princess. You're being **warned**.*"

Silence filled the room.

Then Ilsera stepped closer. "*We understand the prince's charm. His... softness. You've always had a heart, Rachel. That's what made you dangerous. But now, it makes you vulnerable.*"

"*I am not vulnerable,*" Rachel snapped.

"*Then prove it,*" Sorath said. "*Tomorrow morning. A duel. Public. Against the commander of our escort squad.*"

Rachel didn't blink. "*To what end?*"

"*To remind everyone,*" Ilsera said softly, "*that your loyalty lies with **Cerulean steel**, not Indigo silk.*"

Wing IV: Robin Endures

The following morning, Robin woke sore.

Every muscle screamed. His arms felt like stone. His shoulders burned. But he rose anyway.

He arrived in the yard at dawn.

Sir Calder was already there.

"*Good,*" the old man grunted. "*Pain means you're still weak. But not useless*."

Robin forced a grin. "*I'll take that as encouragement*."

"*No,*" Calder said. "*That was encouragement*."

Robin lifted his sword. This time, he did not falter.

Wing V: The Duel of Roses

That same morning, word spread like wildfire through the palace:

Princess Rachel of Cerulean was to duel in the Rose Garden Arena.

The news stunned the summit's guests. Duels were rare at diplomatic summits —

rarer still between visiting royalty and their guards.

Robin heard it during breakfast.

His heart sank.

He left his plate untouched.

Wing VI: Rachel's Blade

In the arena carved from old marble and woven vines, diplomats and soldiers gathered beneath morning mist. The air shimmered with anticipation.

Rachel stepped into the ring, wearing a sleek dueling suit of silver-trimmed leather. Her braid was tight. Her eyes unreadable. In her hand: **Moonfang**, her curved saber, polished and balanced to perfection.

Her opponent, **Commander Veylen**, bowed stiffly. A seasoned fighter with thirty duels behind him and not a single defeat.

Ilsera watched from a raised platform. Varyn sat beside her, arms crossed, unreadable.

The duel began.

Veylen struck fast. His style was aggressive, relentless, meant to pressure and expose.

Rachel countered every blow.

Not with brute strength.

But with precision.

She moved like water flowing, shifting, rebounding. Her blade kissed his gauntlet. Then his shoulder. Then the edge of his collarbone.

And finally, as the crowd hushed, she disarmed him with a pivot and flick that sent his weapon flying.

He fell back, gasping.

Rachel stood still, blade at his throat.

Then she stepped away.

Wing VII: Shadows Remain and Balcony of Doubt

The arena erupted in restrained applause — polite, diplomatic. But among the Cerulean ranks, a wave of reassurance passed through the eyes of commanders and advisors alike.

She had proven herself.

But not all were convinced.

In the shadows, Varyn whispered to a messenger. Another letter was prepared. Another move on the board made.

Later that day, Robin found her on the west balcony, wind tugging at the edges of her sleeves.

"*You won,*" he said softly.

"*I had to.*"

"*You looked like lightning.*"

She turned to him. "*Then why do I feel like I've been struck?*"

He didn't answer at first.

Then: "*Because every time we prove our loyalty to our kingdoms... we carve away a little more of what we could become.*"

Rachel's voice was a whisper. "*Do you think we'll survive this?*"

Robin stepped beside her.

"*If we do," he said, "it'll be because we refused to be anything but ourselves.*"

They stood together, side by side, the wind cold between them.

One trained in steel.

The other is strategy.

Both beginning to realize that the war they feared most... wasn't between nations.

It was within themselves.

8

THE TIDES OF RESISTANCE

By the eighth day of the summit, the tides beneath diplomacy had shifted.

To outsiders, the summit still carried its elegance — banners billowed from castle turrets, harps played beneath chandeliers, and wine was poured as lords and ladies laughed politely.

But beneath the polished surface, **resistance was brewing** quietly, unseen, and dangerously close to ignition.

What neither Robin nor Rachel yet realized was that while they trained to reshape their destinities, their kingdoms had already begun reshaping the battlefield.

Not with swords.

But with **spies.**

Wing I: The Eyes in the Walls

It started with whispers.

In the Indigo kitchens, a cup of wine went undrunk. In Cerulean's embassy wing, a servant went missing for three hours. In a hallway between the observatory and the council chambers, a hidden panel shifted ever so slightly — revealing not dust, but footsteps.

Robin was the first to suspect.

Not because he was paranoid, but because he was a student of patterns — and the patterns had changed. Documents vanished. Messages arrived with different ink strokes. Guards stood too still.

One evening, as he reviewed summit correspondence, he found it.

A duplicate scroll.

Worded the same as one he had read three days earlier. But the wax seal bore **Cerulean script**, not Indigo's.

A forgery.

A planted message.

He brought it to **Commander Elyan** in the dead of night.

"*This was meant to be found,*" Robin said, eyes narrowed. "*Someone is manipulating the flow of information. Possibly from within.*"

Elyan grimaced. "*They're trying to force conflict before the summit ends*."

Robin tapped the scroll. "*This accuses Indigo of plotting a midnight ambush along the Serith Ridge. It's false — but if Cerulean believes it…*"

Elyan finished grimly, "*They'll respond pre-emptively.*"

Wing II: The Eyes in the Walls

At that same hour, **Rachel** stood alone in the Cerulean prayer chamber, a burning message clutched in her hand.

They are deceiving you. Indigo has requested reinforcements for the eastern border. The prince is not what he seems.

The handwriting was Selene's.

Rachel read the words three times before crushing the parchment and tossing it into the brazier.

She paced, Moonfang still belted to her side.

A week ago, she would've believed it.

Now, she wasn't sure of anything — except what she had seen with her own eyes:

Robin, bruised from training, was standing straighter every day. Robin, correcting his nobles without arrogance. Robin, laughing in the garden like someone who had never been allowed to laugh before.

He was changing.

But so was she.

Her nights were no longer filled with certainty. Her dreams, once of battle formations and Cerulean victory, now twisted with images of Robin falling not to her sword, but to betrayal.

Was she betraying Cerulean?

Or was Cerulean betraying her?

Wing III: The Eyes in the Walls

In the quiet of the Indigo archive wing, Robin sat at a desk lit only by candlelight.

He had written her a letter.

Rachel,
I do not know where this ends. But I know where I stand. Not behind Indigo's walls, nor beneath Cerulean's banners — but beside you. If we fall, I would rather fall together than rise divided.

He stared at the ink.

Then folded it. Sealed it.

And placed it under the base of a chess piece in the garden pavilion — a rook, hollowed at its core.

It was the only place he still trusted.

Wing IV: The Eyes in the Walls

Elsewhere, **Lord Varyn** met with an emissary from the southern kingdom of Nareth — a quiet observer at the summit.

The emissary wore green robes and a gold-plated mask.

Varyn offered him a glass of crimson liqueur.

"*The summit drags,*" the emissary said.

"*Because hope is a stubborn weed,*" Varyn replied.

"*You've requested... support?*"

Varyn slid a scroll across the table.

"*In three days, I will present evidence that Indigo has broken the ceasefire agreement. The summit will be thrown into chaos. I want Nareth's fleet poised along the southern coast to respond if war is declared.*"

The emissary sipped slowly. "*A bold move. If it fails...?*"

Varyn's smile was cold. "*Then let fire be our last ambassador.*"

Wing V: The Eyes in the Walls

The next morning, a young courier loyal to Rachel attempted to deliver a private message to Robin.

He never arrived.

Intercepted by Cerulean agents under Lord Varyn's orders, the boy was detained, accused of espionage, and quietly removed from the palace without trial.

The message?

Burned.

Rachel never learned what he carried.

Robin never knew he was waiting for her reply.

The silence between them grew.

But not from choice.

From design.

Wing VI: The Eyes in the Walls

The penultimate meeting of the summit was set for the grand amphitheater, an open forum, attended by all kingdoms, broadcast through magical flame to cities far and wide.

Robin and Rachel were to stand as primary speakers, symbolizing potential unity.

But something felt wrong.

Rachel's guards moved with tighter formation. Robin noticed his father whispering more often with Queen Maria. Ambassadorial staff were sent away early. Backup escorts replaced familiar faces.

And all the while, both Robin and Rachel were wondering the same thing:

Is this still a summit… or the first move of war?

Wing VII: The Eyes in the Walls

The night before the amphitheater address, Robin found a note tucked beneath the chess rook in the garden.

Don't speak tomorrow. You're being set up. Trust no one.
—Rechal

He turned it over. Cerulean wax. Rachel's seal.

No signature.

But he knew her handwriting.

His hands trembled.

He rushed to his study, unrolling map after map, piecing together the implications.

If he stepped up to that podium...

And if the forged documents Varyn had crafted were revealed publicly...

Cerulean could claim **Robin broke the peace**.

A call to arms.

A declaration of betrayal.

A trap.

Robin met with Elyan one last time that night.

"*I could flee,*" he said. "*Vanish from the summit. Delay everything.*"

Elyan shook his head. "*That would only confirm guilt.*"

"*Then what do I do?*"

"*You stand tall,*" Elyan said. "*And trust her.*"

Robin nodded.

Far across the courtyard, Rachel stood on her balcony, gripping the stone railing.

She'd sent the warning.

That was all she could do now.

Any more would brand her a traitor.

She whispered into the wind, hoping it would reach him:

"*Please be careful.*"

The tide was coming.

And neither Indigo nor Cerulean could stop it.

But perhaps, just perhaps, **Robin and Rachel** could learn to swim against it.

9

THE FLAMES OF THE AMPHITHEATER

"When truth burns in silence,
It's the lie that shouts the loudest."

The day had come — the grand address of the summit. Meant to be a culmination of unity, dialogue, and compromise, it was now a stage prepared for manipulation, for the breaking of bonds disguised as formality.

In the great **Amphitheater of Solith**, where kings and queens once spoke of peace after ancient wars, history was about to repeat itself, not with swords, but with twisted words and flaming symbols.

Wing I: Setting the Stage

The amphitheater pulsed with presence. Each step, each voice, echoed through the vast dome. Magic flames burned blue above the banners of the twelve attending nations, casting long shadows down the stone seats where nobles, warriors, diplomats, and emissaries had gathered.

Indigo's delegation wore violet-lined robes, their circlets glinting. Cerulean's party shimmered with white and ocean-blue, proud and tall as they descended.

And at the center, below a gilded arch depicting the ancient gods of diplomacy, stood the twin podiums — carved from marble and obsidian.

One for **Prince Robin of Indigo**. One for **Princess Rachel of Cerulean**.

It was meant to be symbolic.

Unity.

Cooperation.

But both podiums felt like guillotines.

Wing II: Unraveling Threads and The Prince Enters

Rachel arrived first, flanked by her guard and Minister Ilsera. Her heart thudded beneath her ceremonial armor. Moonfang remained sheathed at her back as a silent reassurance.

She scanned the crowd.

Robin was not yet there.

Was he heeding her warning?

Had he fled?

No, that was not the Robin she knew. He would stand, even in a fire.

Her eyes found Lord **Varyn**, sitting three rows above. His face was calm, hands clasped. But his smirk betrayed him.

Something was coming.

The side gates parted.

A hush fell across the amphitheater.

Robin walked through the aisle in a dark cloak, no crown on his head. No guards. No entourage.

Only him.

His eyes locked with Rachel's for a breath.

And she felt the tightness in her chest ease, but only for a moment.

He stopped at the base of the stage.

And climbed.

Wing III: The Speech

The High Chancellor of Thalor, a neutral arbiter, stepped forward.

"*In the name of the gods of earth and sky, we gather to hear the intentions of our youth — heirs to empires, voices of their people. Let truth be spoken, and let peace be judged.*"

He turned.

"*Prince Robin of Indigo.*"

Robin stepped forward. Calm. Controlled.

But inside, thunder.

He drew a folded parchment from his robe. The one he had rewritten five times.

"*I came to this summit to represent my kingdom,*" he began, "*and I will always do so. But I speak not just as a prince — I speak as a man who has walked the quiet halls of strategy and the louder paths of uncertainty.*"

A few murmurs in the crowd.

"*My people are strong in mind. Cerulean is strong in might. And for centuries, that strength has made us fear each other. But fear,*" he paused, "*is a story we've told ourselves too many times.*"

Heads turned. The tension shifted.

"*I do not seek surrender. I do not ask for it. What I offer is understanding. Collaboration. A border council. Rotational command. Shared resources. Shared trust.*"

The chamber stirred again. A few claps echoed, hesitant but hopeful.

Then —

A sharp voice rang out from the Cerulean delegation.

"I object!"

Lord Varyn rose to his feet.

He held up a scroll. Red-sealed. Glowing faintly — enchanted to resist forgery.

"I bring before the summit undeniable proof that Indigo has violated the ceasefire," he said, voice projecting over the murmurs.

Gasps echoed.

Robin froze.

Rachel's stomach dropped.

"This scroll," Varyn continued, *"details orders signed by Queen Maria herself, requesting the secret movement of four battalions to the Serith border — under cover of diplomacy."*

He handed it to the High Chancellor.

"And if that's not treason against the peace," Varyn said, *"I don't know what is."*

The High Chancellor read the scroll aloud. Word for word.

Even the signature matched.

But Robin knew the truth.

It was forged.

Crafted with magic and malice.

Rachel stared, horrified. She recognized the ink. The curve of the signature.

Cerulean's spellmasters were behind it.

Wing IV: The Flames Rise

Shouts erupted.

The Cerulean delegation rose to their feet. Indigo's guards stepped forward. The chancellor tried to quiet the room, but it was too late.

Rachel stepped between the two sides.

"*WAIT!*" she shouted.

Silence struck.

She turned to the assembly. Her voice was steady.

"*I have seen that scroll. I know what it claims. But I have spoken to Prince Robin, I have seen his maps, his orders, his council. There was no such movement. This is a fabrication.*"

Gasps again. From Cerulean.

Ilsera whispered sharply to Varyn: "*She betrays us.*"

But Rachel wasn't done.

"*I accuse no one,*" she said. "*But I ask, what does it say about us if we believe in **papers** more than in people?*"

Robin stepped beside her.

"*For once,*" he said, "*let's not let evidence of fear destroy a chance at peace.*"

Then he reached into his robe and held up a scroll of his own.

A truth spell.

Witnessed. Authorized. Prepared by a neutral kingdom: **Valtheron**, whose mages observed Indigo's records.

He handed it to the Chancellor.

Within moments, a light-blue glow shimmered over the stage. The spell verified:

No movement.

No battalions.

No ceasefire violation.

The forged scroll **burned to ash** in Varyn's hands.

Wing V: The Crowd Reacts

Shock.

Confusion.

And finally, applause.

It started with the Valtheron delegation.

Then Nareth.

Then even the war-hardened envoys of Elaria and Droswen.

A wave of **validation** swept through the amphitheater.

Robin and Rachel stood together, breathing hard, lit by the blue flame of truth.

Wing VI: The Aftermath

Varyn was removed from the chamber under guard. Ilsera vanished before she could be questioned. Cerulean's Queen Mary remained stone-faced.

But her eyes followed Rachel with unease.

Later that evening, Rachel was summoned to her mother's quarters.

Alone.

She went.

Robin returned to his quarters to find Queen Maria waiting.

"*I saw you today,*" she said softly.

"*I thought you might.*"

"*You stood like a king.*"

Robin didn't smile.

"*I stood like a man in love,*" he said.

Maria sighed. "*Then may your love be strong enough to carry the burden of two crowns.*"

Wing VII: The Balcony

That night, Rachel stood alone on the balcony, lit by the moon.

Robin joined her, silent.

"*Do you think we bought peace today?*" she asked.

"*No,*" Robin said. "*But we delayed the war. That's something.*"

She turned to him. "*I want more than delays.*"

He stepped closer.

"*So do I.*"

For a moment, nothing else existed.

Then her hand found his.

Fingers laced.

Not in secrecy. But in **defiance**.

X

THE PRICE OF DEFIANCE

Peace is not merely the absence of war
It is the war fought in silence,
in shadows,
In sacrifices made for love.

They had stood together in the flames.
Now they would face the storm that came after.

Wing I: Ashes of a Summit

The **Amphitheater of Solith**, once resounding with applause and cries of unity, stood deserted.

Charred scrolls. Trampled silk. Abandoned wine goblets. All signs of a summit that had nearly collapsed.

Cerulean's false scroll had been exposed. Varyn disgraced. But the cost of truth was steep.

In the aftermath, trust had fractured—publicly.

And in the privacy of their respective courts, **Robin** and **Rachel** found themselves no longer just heirs.

They were symbols.

Symbols that now threatened old loyalties.

Wing II: Rachel's Ultimatum

Queen Mary's chamber in the Cerulean wing was cold and blue. Glass walls filtered light into fractured shards. Rachel stood before her mother, armor still dusted with ash.

"*You humiliated your court,*" Queen Mary said flatly. "*You saved your enemy.*"

"*I saved the truth.*"

"*You destroyed leverage. Varyn's false proof would have guaranteed us military superiority—*"

"*Through lies!*"

Queen Mary stood slowly, her eyes piercing. "*You are a daughter of Cerulean. Your loyalty is not negotiable.*"

Rachel stepped closer, voice low. "*Then know this. If loyalty requires deception, cruelty, and murder... then it is no longer mine to give.*"

A silence passed between them. Thick. Final.

Queen Mary said nothing as Rachel turned and walked out.

But as the doors shut, she whispered to her councilman, "*Activate* ***the Pale Vow***."

Wing III: The Pale Vow

Deep in the shadows of Cerulean's intelligence chambers, a secret unit was awakened.

The Pale Vow — a faction used only when diplomacy failed, and a target had become too dangerous to live.

They had three directives:

Ensure silence.

Remove the source.

Leave no trace.

Target: ***Prince Robin of Indigo.***

Execution: *Within* ***three nights***.

Wing IV: Robin's Warning

Meanwhile, in the Indigo war room, King Martin and Queen Maria listened to Robin recount every detail from the summit floor.

He spoke with calm clarity. Of Varyn's lie. Rachel's courage. The danger is now brewing.

Maria frowned. "*You realize what this means?*"

Robin nodded. "*They won't stop. We humiliated them in front of twelve kingdoms*."

Martin's eyes darkened. "*Cerulean will not forgive weakness. Or defiance. Especially from one of their own*."

Robin leaned forward. "*Then we can't wait. We must prepare Indigo for war*."

Maria raised an eyebrow. "*You speak like a general*."

Robin met her gaze. "*I don't want to be one. But if I must — let me earn it*."

Wing V: Assassin in Indigo

On the second night after the summit, while bells rang in the western towers for a visiting envoy, a **shadow** slipped into Indigo's palace.

Dressed as a servant.

Name unknown.

Face altered by glamour.

Hands soaked in prior blood.

She crept through corridors, undetected.

She entered Robin's chambers shortly after midnight.

Empty.

She paused.

And then a sharp click. A pressure plate beneath her boot.

A trap.

Steel bars slammed down from the ceiling. Crossbows clicked into place on the walls.

From behind her, Robin emerged, sword drawn. Elyan was by his side.

"*I expected you,*" Robin said coldly.

The assassin said nothing.

She reached for her dagger, but Elyan was faster.

The bolt struck her hand. She screamed. Another pinned her leg.

Robin stepped forward.

"*You're not the last. Are you?*"

Bloodied but defiant, the assassin smirked. "*The Vow does not break.*"

Robin's face darkened.

"*But I will.*"

Wing VI: Rachel's Escape

The next morning, Rachel awoke to find her sword missing.

So was her armor.

And her door locked from the outside.

It wasn't an arrest.

It was a cage.

She understood immediately.

Mary had chosen a path that no longer included her.

But Rachel had trained with the masters of stealth and battlefield survival.

And she remembered the servant tunnels beneath Thalor's guest wing, ancient and unused.

By dusk, she had broken through the wall panel, slipped through the tunnel with nothing but a dagger and a stolen cloak.

She didn't stop until she reached the edge of the Indigo wing.

A guard stepped in her way.

Then paused.

It was **Robin**.

"*I was hoping you'd come,*" he whispered.

She threw her arms around him.

They didn't speak for a long while.

But they understood.

Their kingdoms would no longer shelter them.

And the price of defiance...

Was exile.

Wing VII: Two Against the World

They rode that night two cloaked silhouettes on swift-footed steeds, beneath a sky of cold stars.

Behind them: A trail of betrayal, accusations, and poisoned politics.

Ahead: Uncertainty. Refuge. Possibly death. But also: Hope.

They rode for **Valtheron**, the neutral kingdom that had verified the truth spell. There, perhaps, they could uncover the threads behind The Pale Vow and build a coalition not bound by flags, but by **truth**.

By love.

By conviction.

Rachel rode ahead. Moonfang at her hip. Fierce, focused.

Robin followed, maps and scrolls in his satchel. No longer a boy with ink-stained fingers.

Now, a man with blood on his hands and a fire in his heart.

Wing VIII: The Price Paid

At dawn, they crossed the border.

Their names would be spoken of as traitors.

As lovers.

As threats.

But history would not remember them for how they fled.

It would remind them of what they **returned to do**.

THE END OF
PART - I

UP NEXT

Blades of Indigo-II

Shadows amidst the Flame

ABOUT THE AUTHOR

My self Yatheesha S Pujar, and I come from the quiet town of Challakere. I began writing novels after graduation, inspired by the emotional depth of stories found in both books and anime. What began as a creative outlet soon became my way of connecting with others through shared emotions, struggles, and dreams.

I write romance and fantasy because those genres allow me to explore not just the beauty and magic of the human heart, but also the conflicts and sacrifices that test it. Blades of Indigo was written for anyone who has ever felt torn between duty and desire, who has faced impossible choices, or who has loved someone despite the world being against them.

Through my writing, I hope to move people—to bring tension and triumph where the story demands it, tenderness where the heart needs it, and the hope that even after the fiercest battles, love can still prevail. More than anything, I want readers to know that courage and compassion can change not only lives, but entire worlds.

ACKNOWLEDGMENT

I would like to thank everyone who helped me with the making of Blades of Indigo: Love Amidst Storm.

To my father, Sannapalaiah P A, and my mother, Nirmala S, their bounteous support and blessings have been my strongest pillars, immovable by any storm. I owe them so much love, sacrifices, and motivation to follow my dreams irrespective of all obstacles.

To my sister, Rashmi P S., you continue to spam me about my abilities. My life is brightened by your presence.

This is a novel of love, strength, and imagination, which would not have been possible without the blessings and encouragement of family.

Thank you,

Thanks for reading! Please add a short review on Amazon and let me know what you thought!

www.ingramcontent.com/pod-product-compliance
Ingram Content Group UK Ltd.
Pitfield, Milton Keynes, MK11 3LW, UK
UKHW041317190726
13845UKWH00025B/337

9 789334 360172